Adapted by Emily Skwish

Published by Phoenix International Publications, Inc.
8501 West Higgins Road, Suite 300, Chicago, Illinois 60631
Lower Ground Floor, 59 Gloucester Place, London W1U 8JJ
www.pikidsmedia.com

p i kids is a trademark of Phoenix International Publications, Inc.,
and is registered in the United States.
Look and Find is a trademark of
Phoenix International Publications, Inc.,
and is registered in the United States and Canada.

8 7 6 5 4 3 2 1

ISBN: 978-1-5037-2583-6

PJMASKS

pi kids

phoenix international publications, inc.

Into the night to save the day! Can you find these heroes and baddies battling in the museum?

Catboy

Gekko

Owlette

Romeo

Luna Girl

Night Ninja

FIND THE FACES

Review the pages and find two faces that are exactly the same:

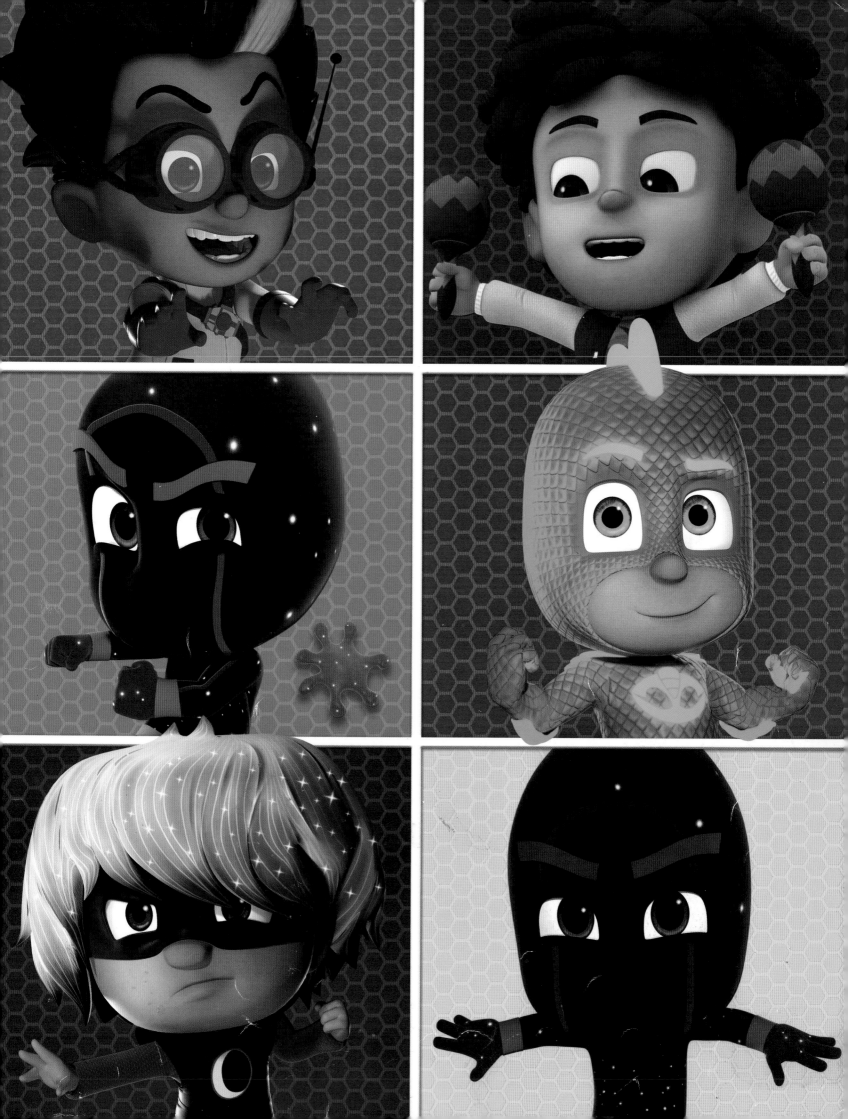

Night Ninja and his Ninjalinos want to take over Catboy's HQ! Can you spot them before they succeed?

Ninjalino 1

Ninjalino 2

Ninjalino 3

Night Ninja

Ninjalino 4

Ninjalino 5

FIND THE HEROES

Look carefully and find both the daytime kids AND the nighttime superheroes! Can you locate Connor and Catboy, Amaya and Owlette, and Greg and Gekko? Watch out for baddies along the way!

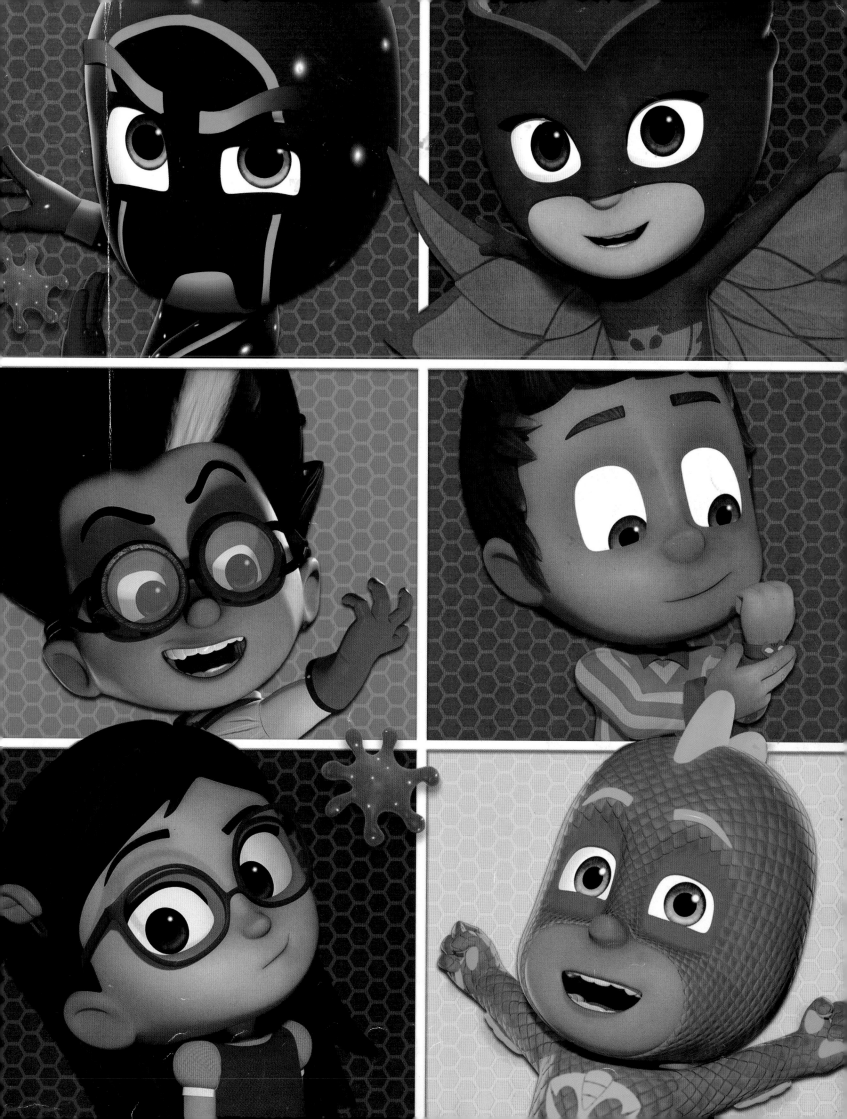

The PJ Masks and the nighttime super villains have lots of tricks and tools to help them save—or ruin—the day! See if you can find these:

Luna Magnet

Pogo Dozer

Owl Glider

Gekko camouflage

Luna Board

Cat-Car

In the nighttime, the PJ Masks battle baddies in their supercars. But in the daytime, Connor, Amaya, and Greg zip and zoom on their super-cool bikes. While the friends pedal, look around for these other things they play with under the sun:

tennis rackets

soccer ball

toy helicopter

jump rope

drum

skateboard

Museum starts with m. Zip back to the museum and find these other things that start with m:

- mask
- moths
- microphone
- mad scientist
- moon

Nighttime is the right time for stargazing. Motor back to the vehicles and find 20 shining stars!

Fly back to the Find the Faces page and point to someone who is:

- next to **Catboy**
- under **Owlette**
- over **a Ninjalino**
- between **Owlette and Cameron**
- below **Gekko**
- above **Night Ninja**

Creep back to Catboy's HQ and find these shapes:

Uh-oh! Night Ninja has been here! Swoosh

Slink back to the baddies and sidekicks and find a character who:

has fluttery wings

wears a white lab coat

flies on a Luna Board

is a martial arts expert

wears a black costume

is a mini-version of one of the baddies

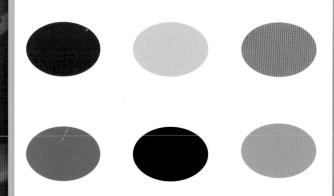

Go back to the Find the Heroes page and look for clothes in these colors:

Night and flight are words that rhyme. Go back to the PJ Masks HQ and find things that rhyme with the words below:

ridge (bridge)

daughter (water)

zero (hero)

spoon (moon)

sing (wing)

bee (tree)

You can't spell bike without the letter b! Pedal back to the daytime and find these other things that start with the letter b:

balloon

basketball

bird

book

bench

butterfly

through all the pages and find 20 sticky splats he left behind!